James O'Leary

Ellie Laura

The border orphan

James O'Leary

Ellie Laura
The border orphan

ISBN/EAN: 9783337340247

Printed in Europe, USA, Canada, Australia, Japan

Cover: Foto ©Andreas Hilbeck / pixelio.de

More available books at **www.hansebooks.com**

ELLIE LAURA;

OR,

THE BORDER ORPHAN.

A DRAMA.

By Rev. JAMES O'LEARY, D. D.

NEW YORK:

P. O'SHEA, 27 BARCLAY STREET.

P. DONAHOE, FRANKLIN STREET, BOSTON.

J GRAHAM, MADISON STREET, CHICAGO.

PRICE ONE DOLLAR.

DRAMATIS PERSONÆ.

TERESA,
STANISLAUS,
CONSTANTIA, } Nuns.
IRENE,
ELLIE LAURA, the Border Orphan.
CLARA, an Illinois Girl.
ESTA, a Massachusetts Girl.
IDA, a New York Girl.

SHABNAYE, an Indian Chief.
SHE-BUFFALO, a Squaw.
WALLA-WALLA, } Papooses.
WINA,
McSHANE, Colonel.
FATHER TOM.
CROTTY, } Settlers.
KINSELLA,

DELIA, AGNES, MARIA, ETHEL, ANNA,
ANASTASIA, JULIA, JANE, HANNA, } Pupils.
CORA, EULALIA, WINNIE, ANGELINA,

PREFACE.

This drama was written for the pupils of St. Joseph's Academy, Brooklyn, E. D.

It is an attempt to meet a demand for amusement and instruction in Catholic educational institutions.

There are but three scenes ; one in a schoolroom, one by the bank of a river, and one in an Indian wigwam. The drama is founded on fact, the saving of the white settlers along the Illinois river by Shabnaye during the Black Hawk war. Ellie Laura is a fictitious character and a representative of the sufferings, the vicissitudes, and the combinations that have taken place in settling our vast Western country. The plot, the characters, and the moral of this drama, are remitted to the judgment of the public, and may be found to possess a living interest for the inhabitants of Illinois along the Illinois river. The songs have been set to music by a Sister of St. Joseph's Academy.

As this drama was written at the request of Rev. S. Malone, Pastor of Sts. Peter and Paul's Church, Brooklyn ; to him it is dedicated, with a hope that it will remain a witness of his good heart, clear head, and deep sense of principle.

Rev. Dr. J. O'Leary.

Brooklyn, January 26, 1872.

PROLOGUE.

An Acrostic to Rev. Sylvester Malone.

Rise and come, gentle hearers, with me to the West,
Enchantingly follow the sun to his rest,
View the wild prairie spread and wild buffalo roam,
See the forests arise from the deep precious loam
Yclad in the grandeur of age and of joy—
Looking proud by the rivers of proud Illinois!

View the mountains uprise and in majesty grow,
Enrobed with the forest and crowned with the snow!
Sun-silvered the woodland, by the broad stream and blue.
The deer, and the elk, and the bear hides from view ;
Encumbered by naught and far wilder than these,
Rude Indians fashion their wigwams of trees.

Mellifluous ringeth the prairie winds' strain,
And liberty loveth the sky-bounded plain ;
Lo! Liberty, chainless, pure spirit of light,
O'er the wide prairie wanders encircled with might !
Now, then, come, gentle folks, to the wild West with me,
Ellie Laura, the lost border orphan to see.

ELLIE LAURA.

SCENE I.

In a Schoolroom at Morris, Ills.

Ellie Laura soliloquizing.

Here, in the wilds of distant Illinois,
There is a sadness indescribable,
Which, day by day, and year by year, to me
Has clung and deepens—yet I know not how!
Friends—I have ; and Religion lifts her shield
To guard me, and consoles me with a balm
And gentle judging kindness, which not aught
Of earth begets.   Religion follows me,
Fans me, soothes me, and consolations bright
Sheds round me, hoping to impart some cheer,
Some joy of lasting kind ; but settled gloom
And sense of sorrow irremovable,
Press on me inwardly.   Am I alone ?
From the unseen recesses of my heart,
A melancholy mist of thoughts exhales
To ever vapor and bedew my brain.
Am I in company ?   The sunshine fair

Of fair companions' faces, rests on me
As beams upon the deep and troubled sea.
In prayer there is a sombre quietness,
An unfulfilled and scarcely tasted sweet,
That in the boundless void, where shapeless sprites
Inhabit, hapless beings be as I.
But how know I what is, or is to be,
Away in that impenetrable void?
Why fly from what I see and most admire
To seek a solace of phantastic form ?
The past is changeless, changeless what to come ;
Time as a river flows, and by the stream
Of my existence is a margin, marred
With thoughts which now recede and now approach,
As bluffs that grimly guard the banks
Of yon blue, deep, wide-sweeping Illinois.
Time was, in younger years of my young life,
When all was undisturbed and unobscured,
As where Mirooka sees yon prairie plain.
Has thou no charms, O Morris? Kankakee !
Canst thou not send some gentle breeze to breathe
Aroma rife with spells?   From Fox, fair stream
Of lovely vales, where sweet Aurora smiles,
Is there no welcome gale?   Ye virgin leas,
Ye unmolested and untrodden groves,
Ye boundless wilds, ye prairie-wandering streams,
Whose magic life and spell my spirit feels,
Can ye not make my sullen spirit smile ?
Or did I wander from the far East—

Enters Sister Teresa.

Sister Teresa,   Dear child,
    It is a glorious morning. Oh! There is
An exquisite calm reigning everywhere.
No clouds of treacherous form are visible—
The air abroad no murky aspect wears,
But a serenely sweet bewitching smile
Laughs on the face of nature : and, anon,
What with delightful weather, with superb
Scenery, and, it may be, with some new
Romantic incidents—what with our mates
Exultant and rejoicing by the stream,
Think you not, Ellie Laura, we shall have
A glorious day in our excursion trip ?

Ellie Laura.   Surely. It will much glad my many friends.
    The pupils long expectant speak thereof
With much enthusiasm, and not unmixed
With prayer that all will prove a great success.

Teresa.   Ellie, it must delight you much, being so
    Congenial to your own disposition.

Ellie Laura.   Assuredly. I feel a secret charm
    In this wild western country ; as if God
Had made it Eden-like, and honored us,
Its first inhabitants (the roaming tribes
We mark not) by here gathering, planting us.
I love its newness, wildness, fruitfulness,
Its greatness, unapproached magnificence—
They always glad me so.

Teresa.   Your classmates, too.

Ellie Laura. Esta is pleased : I saw her yesterday.
    Clara I met this morning by the way—
    She is delighted. Ida jumps with joy.
    The rest you soon will see ; and as for me—

Enters a class of children.

Teresa. I wish you all a happy holiday.
All answer. Thanks ? Thanks, dear Sister !
Teresa.   I shan't spend your time
    This morning ; when religious exercise
    Is ended, ye depart.
All.   Thanks, Sister, thanks !
Teresa. Which is the morning verse to Christ, our Lord ?
Esta and three others.

    O Christ, Almighty King of Kings,
    Before all ages born,
    Whose light from light its splendor flings
    O'er Sion's cloudless morn—
Teresa. To Mary, Virgin ?
Clara and three others.

    O Queen of grace and peerless power,
    Bright mirror of the Word,
     Of Sion's gate unconquered tower—
    Hail, Mother of the Lord !
Teresa.   To Saint Patrick, next,
    Apostle of Ierne of the streams ?
Delia and three others.

    O Patrick, Ireland's glorious Paul !
    O father ever blest !

O glorious son of glorious Gaul!
Great Primate of the West!

Teresa. Children, what is your prayer to Ireland's saint?

All. While grow the trees,
While blows the breeze,
While water seeks the sea,
His Faith with us may be!

Teresa. To Mary, Virgin, and to Christ, our Lord?

All. O Mother, pray for us in every strife!
O Jesus, grant us everlasting life!

Teresa. Let us, to-day, by our appointment state,
Concise and clear, what Holy Church enjoins,
What doctrines mould the Catholic intellect,
What laws the Christian will must needs obey,
Why human minds to Heaven's decrees must bow.
Say, Clara, first—whence springs the light that sheds
Its rays resistless on the human soul?

Clara. Two lights illumine man. There is the light
Which reason, the Creator's mirror, shows;
There is the light two Revelations write:
These lights from Light, are not, nor can be foes.
In characters indelible and bright,
From them the laws for mind and will arose;
Sealed with the seal of God before all time began,
No age, no change know they. Two lights illumine
man.

Teresa. But since in Revelation mysteries
There are, high and incomprehensible;
Which, Ida, tell are those we needs must know?

Ida. Throughout the Roman universal fold,

Five mysteries, principal, we hold :
One only God and Triune 'fore all time,
That God Incarnate, dead, from death sublime ;
To God, the Father, Son, and Holy Ghost,
All worship due from man and angels' host !

Teresa. Will Ellie Laura please explain the laws—
The ties of love that lie twixt us and God ?

Ellie Laura. Alas ! how weak and worthless we,
Pale creatures of pale misery,
High children of high destiny !
Praise to the Lord alone !

Doth not each wight, that crawls through time,
Since born of God, though out of slime,
In oneness show the One sublime ?
Praise to the Lord alone !

Doth not the immortal spirit pass
Heavenward from its earthly mass,
And let it moulder as the grass ?
Praise to the Lord alone !

Humanity in coffins pent
Groaned Abba, till the Father sent
His Son, and rent that tenement :
Praise to the Lord alone !

The Son appeared, like as the day,
And on lost man outpoured His ray
To recreate created clay :
Praise to the Lord alone !

And when the Son had built the dome,
He sent the Spirit to His Home,
Within the deathless Church of Rome :
Praise to the Lord alone !

We are of God—to God we go ;
From Christ all grace, all truth must flow ;
Shall we not in Christ's Spirit grow,
And praise the Lord alone ?

All.   We praise the Lord alone !

Teresa. Now, the Ten Laws unto the Hebrews given
    With signs of darkness, mist, and cloud, and light,
    And on the Mount interpreted by Christ,
    Last, as ten pillars of the moral code,
    And bind the will of man.   The Sacraments,
    As streams, flow through the city of the soul,
    And sound the seven voices of the Lord,
    Murmuring musically.   Sacrifice,
    Prayer, good deeds, penances, as incense, rise
    From all good Catholics unto God's throne,
    Lovely as melting mists in mellow morn.
    But how do Catholics unto the Lord
    The homage of the intellect declare ?

Delia. By faith.

Rosa.   By the Creed.

Teresa.   There are many creeds ;
    Some made by Councils, some by Fathers, some
    By Popes.   Of the Apostles one is named,

Which doth consist of twelve short articles,
Each framed by one of the twelve chosen chiefs.
Let twelve the parts of the twelve chiefs declare.

Agnes for Peter. I, Peter, do this testimony bear :
There is one God o'er heaven, and earth, and air ;
All things from Him, Almighty Father, spring—
The viewless, deathless, uncreated King.

Teresa. Next.
The Lord is love, and love is light ;
Eternal Light, the Father's sheen,
With boundless love and boundless might,
Is made the Christ—I, John, have seen.

Teresa. Third.

Ethel for James. Hail, Mother Mary, full of grace !
From thee by Spirit's shadowing face
Impregned, His birth Christ claims.
This is the witness of St. James.

Teresa. Fourth.

Ann for Andrew. When Roman Pilate ruled the Jew,
The cross was lifted for a throne ;
And Christ his blinded people slew—
I, Andrew, saw His tomb of stone.

Teresa. Fifthly, Anastasia.

Anastasia for Philip. The Christ descended to the **dead,**
Glad tidings to the saints to bring ;
On the third day, resurgent Jesus led
The imprisoned, as their heavenly King.

Teresa.   Sixth article.

The Lord in glory heavenward rose,

And captive led His vanquished foes ;

On God's right hand He sits on high :

These truths I believe, though Thomas I.

Teresa.   Which is the seventh, say ?

Jane for Bartholomew.   Woe ! woe to the nations ! Woe ! woe to the Jew !

For all nations shall wail and the Lord's day shall rue,

And Jesus will judge both the living and dead.

Yea ! This is the truth which Bartholomew said.

Teresa.   What saith St. Matthew, the Evangelist ?

Hannah for Matthew.   The Holy Spirit, Vivifying **Mas-**ter see—

The Third and Holy Person of the Trinity.

Teresa.   Cora, what saith St. James of Alpheus?

Cora for St. James.   St. James one, holy Church, **and** Catholic, defined,

And Saints communion not by this world's sphere confined.

Teresa.   St. Simon?

Delia for St. Simon.   The church hath power men's **sins** to bind and unbind.

Teresa.   And St. Jude?

Winnie for St. Jude.   Arise ! arise, ye dead, from **out** the grave,

Be clothed with the frames ye knew before—

Teresa.   Mathias, last ?

Angelina for Mathias. What part the Christ, as judge, in
    judgment gave—
    Or joys or woes ; that hold ye ever more,

Teresa. These are the truths, a gracious Saviour brought
    From viewless worlds ; and His disciples' words
    Have spells, as memory of music loved.
    Like chimes of distant bells, they sound all time,
    At morn, at noon, at eventide, and call
    Us from this world away—home, ever home.
    The friend that solaces the broken heart,
    The child that soothes the tear of mother's woe,
    The traveller bearing wealth and knowledge home,
    The bowels of mercy, and the balm of hearts
    Full and overflowing with benevolence ;
    These have charms, but round the Saviour's name
    Their rays concentrate to one living flame.
    Ere you depart, to Christ, the Saviour pray.

All. O Christ, the Saviour ! prolong our days,
    O Virgin Mother, Mary ! guard our ways,
    O Patrick ! warm our hearts with living rays
    Of love, to ever sing the Saviour's praise !
    (*Exeunt Omnes.*)

SCENE II.

In the Country by the River Illinois.

She Buffalo. Wina, come hither. Walla Walla, come,
    I wish to talk of times long since gone by.

Wina. She Buffalo!

Walla Walla. She Buffalo!

She Buffalo. Sit here.

Look towards the river. I have often heard,
When I was small, Shabnaye's great-grandfather
Said, this whole vale was by the river filled
From hill to hill. The waters washed yon heights.
Pale faces never saw that great, great sight.
But that was many hundred moons ago.
And yonder, one day's walk along the stream,
There are big heaps of earth with many dead.
Their bones would build the homes of all the Whites.
The heaps are on the hills. The Indians came.
When ice was on the stream from hill to hill,
And walked across to see the big, big bones—
The big, big skulls of our old Indian braves.
In coming from the lands where sets the sun,
They counted many moons. They brought with them
Dead braves, dead squaws, and dead papooses too.
They looked up to the heavens, and in right line
Walked by the stars. Big fires blazed on the heights,
Like the red sun at eve. From yonder heights
The Red man goes to the far hunting grounds.
Wina and Walla Walla, never stir
The bones or skulls within those heaps of earth ;
For the Great Spirit guards the Indians there.
But always do what says She-Buffalo.
Shabnaye is hunting bears. Sing songs for me.

Walla Walla.　　I sing a song that's old one thousand
　　　　moons ;

Song.

On desert and on mountain,
By river and by stream,
Where glows the silver fountain
And glistens the bright beam—
In the west, in the west far away,
Sings the Red man as dieth the day
There is nought like the land of Shabnaye !

For prairies, streams, and wildwood,
For bull, and bear, and deer,
For nature's fairest childhood
The buffalo to cheer—
In the west, in the west far away,
Sings the Red man as dieth the day,
There is nought like the land of Shabnaye !

The blue bird chirps so sweetly,
And whoops the whippowill,
And coos the chicken meetly,
And sips the duck its fill ;
In the west, in the west far away,
Sings the red man as dieth the day,
There is nought like the land of Shabnaye !

She-Buffalo.　　'Tis not so now.　Where the white man
　　　　appears,
　　The Red man must leave.　The bear, the deer,

The prairie chicken, and the buffalo
Follow the sun with the Red man to the West.
White man comes with the morning from the East,
Like grasshoppers.   We go to night and death.
Yet linger we by yonder heaps of earth,
Where Red man sleeps for thousands of full moons.
Wina, sing you the hymn of the dead braves.

Song.

Wina.   Great spirit of the wind and hill,
      Whose voice is heard in storms;
      Bright be the grounds where Buffalo Bill
      His tents and wigwams forms !
      Great spirit of the thunder-cloud,
      Whose fire is Red at night;
      Swift be the steed, and war-dance proud
      Of brave, but dead, Red Light!

      And Red Light had a noble squaw,
      She sleeps in yonder mound ;
      Sweet be thy sleep, brave Mineha,
      In happy hunting ground !
      Great spirit of the Red man's lands,
      To thee the Red men pray ;
      Great spirit ! hear, when Red man stands
      By tombs of brave Shabnaye !

She-Buffalo.   When I go to the happy hunting grounds,
   Do not forget these songs.   You think of me.
   I learned them, when I was papoose like you.
   Ho ! Ho ! Shabnaye ! Shabnaye !

Papooses.   Shabnaye!

Shabnaye.   She-Buffalo, papooses, stand ye still.
  I hunted miles beyond our home—away
  Beyond our home where Highland is—away
  In Indian land.   Met deer, met buffalo,
  Killed deer, killed buffalo, killed elk, killed birds,
  In Black Hawk's lands.   Black Hawk with all his
        braves
  Is on the war-path.   Crouching Bear with him.
  Blue Button, Black Cap, Spotted Tail, Wa-Wa,
  Wild Horse, Big Mountain, Wasatch, Goring Bull,
  With all their braves in paint, come like the wind.
  They kill the white man, white papoose, white squaw.
  Two weeks I came, fast as the sun, to tell
  The White man hide.   Like prairie fire, they come.
  The fire of burning houses, like red clouds
  From world's end to world's end.   I killed a bear
  Near our own wigam by the Illinois.
  Wina' and Walla-Walla, rest ye here.
  She-Buffalo brings food and seeks the woods.
  I tell the Black Gown and his Sisters hide.

  Exeunt Shabnaye and She-Buffalo, Shabnaye shouting.

    Whites! the Red man fight his way,
    Whites! the Red man ne'er betray,
    Whites! Shabnaye, your friend Shabnaye,
    Never bend the knee.

Papooses.   Let us go too.   Let us go too.   Quick! quick!
  Exeunt papooses.

Enter Sisters Stanislaus, Constantia, and Irene.

Stanislaus. Now all is ready for the day and guests.
  The children with their friends will soon be here,
  And well it fares with little waifs thus far.
  Constantia, did you see papooses here ?
Constantia. I did. They fled, like hares, at our approach ;
  Their manners are so rude. Reared in the wilds,
  And nothing knowing of cultured life—poor things !—
  Why not their habits a wild impress wear ?
  What bird will on the branch thy presence wait ?
Irene. They are papooses of Shabnaye. Awhile
  And we shall see them, and, it may be, Shabnaye
  Himself, and his good squaw, She-Buffalo.
  From time to time, they come to sell eggs, fish,
  Birds, meat, fruit, vegetables, and the like.
  They pluck wild flowers and form them into wreaths
  Of shapely form and sweetest fragrancy.
  I have seen moccasins, inlaid with beads,
  And worked with skill surpassing the far East.
  Shabnaye, She-Buffalo, and all his tribe,
  Are friendly Indians.
Stanislaus.   Oh ! that they remained ?
Irene. They know right well our Black Gown, Father
      Tom.
  At times the Indians have a feast. They dance,
  They yell, sing war-songs and if possible—
Constantia. Do what ?
Irene.   Get drunk and leave some one to watch—
Constantia. Watch what ?

Irene.   Why, watch without a drink at all,
  And under strictest pain of life.   Next time,
  The watchman will be free.

Stanislaus.   It is a shame,
  A degradation of America,
  To brutalize the savage, and instil
  Into his rude and undeveloped soul,
  The passions that true Christian manhood stain.
  I'd much more rather be a wild Red Man,
  With nature rude and uncontaminate,
  Than a foul pestilential poison thus!
  The wild Red man may roam the darkest woods—
  They speak to him of God and liberty!
  The wild Red man, or swims or floats the stream—
  It ennobles and lifts him up to God!
  The wild Red man surveys the prairie wide—
  Its outspreading expanse swells him to God!
  There is a something grand and undefined,
  An innate and exalted effluence,
  A spirit that bestirs the elements,
  Shed over this wide hemisphere and wild,
  And mantles o'er the Red man's brow with pride.

Irene. You, Stanislaus, are always serious;
  Know you not what She-Buffalo has done?

Constantia. Did what ?

Irene.   She skinned a gopher, and as fish
  Sold it to the Black Gown.

Stanislaus.   Untrue!   Untrue!

Irene. That's so.   The other day, she, likewise, said

She saw Black Gown, a man with small brown eyes,
Hooked nose, and shoulders like a buffalo,
Barefoot, and jumping with a long, long pole
From cake to cake of ice along the Illinois.

Stanislaus. Enough! Enough!

Irene.   Yes! She said she had seen
    A big dead bear upon his back; and he
    Went barefoot, walking straight like her Shabnaye.

Enter Black Gown, Ellie Laura, Clara, Esta, Ida and many
more.

Black Gown. We sought you through the fields, and met
    at last.

    How's Stanislaus? Constantia? How Irene?

Irene. Now, 'tis the month of May
    And all the earth is gay.

Black Gown. I met Teresa and the rest. Success —
    Yes! Yes! to-day is surely a success.
    The young ones seem so bright, so satisfied.
    Even old folks look gay and glad to-day.
    What is the matter with this gentle girl?
    Alone she seems so settled and so sad.

Stanislaus. Perhaps, she may the cause in verse explain.

Ellie Laura. To know is mine, but to assuage in vain.

Song.

    I am a lone and orphan child,
    And I am sad as few:
    When young, my home was in the wild
    That skirts sweet Avondhu.

And I was forced to cross the main
And wander to the West,
Till wandering on I found it vain
To find one spot of rest.

No fields, no flowers, no streams, no skies,
Can paint or bless the view,
Since there's a spell for me where lies
My home by Avondhu.

My mother lives by foreign shore,
Or moulders by the main ;
My father I shall see once more,
Unless my hope is vain.

I am a lone and orphan child,
And I am sad as few ;
When young, my home was in the wild
That skirts sweet Avondhu.

Black Gown. In the old land there are three Avondhus ;
Is there a trio for America ?

Trio's Song.—(Clara, Esta, Ida.)

Clara for Illinois. My home is in proud Illinois,
And I extol the West :
My heart exults and calls with joy,
My home the home of rest.

Repeated by trio.

Esta for Massachusetts. Where Massachusetts stems the sea,
 Upon the beaten shore—
  There is the home of liberty,
  The home that I adore.

Repeated by trio.

Ida for New York. The Hudson forms a noble bay,
 The sister of proud Cork ;
  My heart and soul are in the lay
  That swells to grand New York !

Repeated by trio.

Black Gown. I hear some noise abroad, as that of fear—

Enter Teresa, Crotty, Kinsella, McGennis, and others.

Teresa. We come on sad and sudden circumstance :
 Black Hawk is on the war-path ! Sudden rise,
 Sudden haste to dark woods, and sudden hide !
 Some to Shabnaye and some to Kinsella—

Black Gown. Good God! what sudden, dire calamity!
 O Lord ! show forth Thy power, protect Thy friends !
 No night but knows the rising of a day—

All depart saying,

 O God ! soon show the rising of that day !

SCENE III.

In Shabnayé's Wigwam.

Ellie Laura soliloquizing. Alas ! O that the men were
  never born,
 Who built the ship that hither wafted me !

O would the waves had swallowed her at sea,
And thus anticipated this my doom!
O had I perished in my younger days,
And had not lived to taste of trials thus!
Ah! that my mind had slept in infant form ;
And sorrow after sorrow had not swept
Across my path to bend me to the earth,
A weeping willow looking on the grave!
Ah! well-a-day! Again.   Ah! well-a-day!

Enter Papooses.

Papooses. Don't mourn, don't mourn. She-Buffalo not
pleased.

Walla Walla. We always do what says She-Buffalo.

Wina. She-Buffalo will soon be here again.

Walla Walla. And, then, we all be glad—

Papooses.   We all be glad.

Ellie Laura. Ah! were my heart as blithe and uncon-
cerned

As that which in your little bosoms heaves,
And were I, gentle little Indians, born
In forests, and in forests reared from youth ;
Like you, with hearts unthinking and unawed,
Heedless, light-hearted, playful, I would be.
The birds' sweet song, as heavenly melody,
Would ring by deep, wide-sweeping Illinois.
Entranced I would the live-long day remain,
And wander by its banks, and see the beams
Dance on its eddies, and wild birds approach

Its face with kisses and with outspread wings,
And fishes frolicsome along its waves.
And the calm roseate face of forest morn,
With all its freshness and its noiseless charms,
Would be to me delightful ; and at eve
The setting sun, with golden canopy,
And fair embroidery of silver hue,
Above and round his far horizon throne,
Shedding effulgence, effluence, and balm,
Afar o'er stream, and wood, and plain, and lake—
Ah! such to me enchantment were, to make
The bear's roar sweet, the wolf's howl musical :
Ah! well-a-day! Again. Ah! well-a-day!

Papooses. Don't mourn, don't mourn. She-Buffalo not
pleased.

Wina. She-Buffalo soon come.

Walla Walla. Sing songs.

Papooses Sing songs.

Ellie Laura. Song.

Oh! I met with two angels in woodland all wild ;
Heavenly beauty their countenance wore,
And they strove to console a disconsolate child,
And alas! it grew worse than before.
The light which they shed but increased the deep
gloom
Of that child's weary life and its pain ;
Since its sorrows had marked it a child of the tomb,
And to strive to console it were vain.

Then the two little angels looked up to the sky,
And spoke of the joys that are there :
"Must thou grieve, gentle child, while those man-_
    sions on high
Look so splendid, so happy, so fair ?"
" No, no," said the child, " with bright wings I shall go
From the earth with its sorrow and gloom ;
This one joy I must have in the depth of my woe,
Though I am a child of the tomb."

Papooses. She-Buffalo soon come. She pleased. She
    pleased.

Papooses.

Duette on the Gopher

Down by the stream,
At morning beam,
The happy little gopher
Came on his way
To find some prey,
Like any other loafer
At early morn,
Hard by the corn,
The two of us were playing,
And, when we saw
His little paw,
We stayed where we were staying.
Oh ! the gopher,
The dear and happy gopher !

Caught at morn
Hard by the corn,
Our happy little gopher!

With teeth he chips
Outside his lips,
As sharp as any other ;
And with big cheeks
He loudly squeaks,
He wants his little brother ;
But in the ground
He'll ne'er be found
As long as we are able—
But he'll be fed,
Just near our bed,
Beneath our little table.
Oh! the gopher,
The dear and happy gopher!
Caught at morn,
Hard by the corn,
Our happy little gopher!

Papooses. Heigh! heigh! She-Buffalo! She-Buffalo!
She mourn, she mourn—papoose with the pale face.
She-Buffalo. Poor white papoose, hear me. I have a heart.
When brave Shabnaye comes back, we have good
news.
Shabnaye was on the war-path many times—
As many times as days are in one moon.
He always comes with scalps of brave and squaws.

Likewise this time he comes with many scalps.

Let us pow-wow. Be brave like Indian squaw.

Ellie Laura. Would that my soul were made of harder
    stuff!

The rock wears by the trickling of a drop;

'Tis time my face were furrowed by its tears.

Scarce had I laughed to my fond mother's smile,

When I was from her bosom torn away,

And wafted o'er a wide and angry sea,

To grow 'mong strangers in a foreign clime,

Like plants in sunshine born and from light taken.

Again, to father lost, and orphan found,

And hurried from companionship and friends

To new companionship, new friends, new homes,

What, save religion, was there to me left?

After e'er changing and e'er losing life,

What now confronts me, but a home in woods,

Surrounded by wild beasts and wilder men?

Ah! well-a-day! Again. Ah! well-a-day!

She-Buffalo. The White man thinks the Red man has no
    heart.

We have good, kindly hearts. We know our wrongs.

We feel hard deeds, and do not wail as you.

We've lost our lands. Away from the far East,

We have been driven towards the setting sun.

We have not buffalo, elk, deer, birds, fish,

As we used have. We're always growing few,.

Like leaves of trees of forests in the Fall;

We have brave Indian hearts, and do not mourn.

We Indians have good eyes, big strength, kind hearts
Before the White man, and we must perform
His works, and do his will, and do not mourn.
Poor, white papoose!   I will take care of you ;
I have a kind, good heart—Oh! do not mourn!

E lie Laura. Ah, me!   I would I might not mourn,
    But I must mourn again,
     Since I was from a father torn,
    And mother mourn in vain.

    And two lost brothers I deplore—
    Their loss would melt a stone ;
    And I must mourn, and mourn the more,
    That I am now alone.

    Misfortunes now my joys destroy,
    And I love nought I hail ;
    Here in the land of Illinois,
    My joy is endless wail.

She-Buffalo. Ho! Ho! Here are three white papooses.   See!

Ellie Laura. Hail! ye companions of my woe,
    Can ye in sorrows joy?
    Can ye, with me, all hopes forego
    And wail through Illinois?

    Though fortune presses woe on woe,
    As darkly as the night ;
    In all its darkness there's a glow—
    Companianship is light!

The trio.

Clara. No tribulations shall destroy
          Our hopes of good, our hopes of joy,
          Or make us wail through Illinois
          Endlessly.

Repeated by the trio.

Esta. No terrors ought a coward make,
          No woes a pure soul's manhood break,
          Nor should a noble spirit quake
          Needlessly.

Repeated by the trio.

The Polar night knows equal day.
We hope in God, we trust Shabnaye,
And dark calamities survey
Fearlessly.

Repeated by the trio.

She-Buffalo. Brave ! brave ! papooses, how have ye es-
          caped ?

Esta. Escaped !—why, we directly sought the woods,
          There to await the passing of the storm ;
          When Black Hawk's bands were known to be at war,
          Bounding like buffaloes behind Shabnaye,
          Some screamed, some wept, some prayed, and some
                despaired.
          There was no time to lose. Now, one long night,
          At times in anxious thought, at times in fear,
          Is passed. The luncheon for our holiday

We changed to rations, and the wood as walls
Rose wild and dark around us, and the moss
As pillow served, and stars were hung as lamps
In the pale sky above us, and our home
Was solitude, and our defense was God.

Ida. Yea! even when from the dense underbrush,
Where we lay hidden, we beheld the smoke
Of burning houses blackly cloud the sky,
And when we heard the wierd war-whoop of fiends
Madly pursuing their way as raging wolves,
And when we saw their fires on yonder heights
Shining at dead of night, while round them rode
Chieftains with painted faces, and bedecked
With plumes, and blazing scarlet, and bright blue.

Clara. But we were sad—lamenting, it may be,
The death of our dear mates and our fond friends.
For them we mourned much more than for ourselves;
And thy fate, Ellie Laura, crossed our minds.

Ellie Laura. It is not home nor life I mourn,
Nor things that glad the eye,
For since I was from a father torn,
I do not pause to die.

Ida. And now the war-tide of Black Hawk is passed.
His trail was westward—ever westward. Ho!
This morn, as rose the sun, he left yon heights
And highlands for the far Mississippi;
Crotty we met, who sent us to Shabnaye.

She-Buffalo. The war trail now is o'er,
 Black Hawk will come no more,
 Nor Wa-Wa paint with gore :
 Rejoice! rejoice! rejoice!

 Wild Horse, nor Crouching Bear,
 Nor Goring Bull, will wear
 The White squaw's flowing hair :
 Rejoice! rejoice! rejoice!

 Of all the Reds that stray
 Along the forest way,
 There's none like brave Shabnaye :
 Rejoice! rejoice! rejoice!

 Unequalled in the fray,
 Unable to betray,
 There's none like brave Shabnaye :
 Rejoice! rejoice! rejoice!

 With many scalps to day,
 Home—home returns all gay,
 Shabnaye, the brave Shabnaye
 Rejoice! rejoice! rejoice!

   Enter Crotty and Kinsella.

Crotty. So, so She-Buffalo. You are all here.
 Well, that is good. These young ones are all safe.
 So are all, all. Black Hawk has missed his mark.
 Two companies of Union troops are come.

Kinsella. Though we have lost some houses, it is well
 Our scalps are safe : we owe it to Shabnaye.

Enters Shabnaye.

Shabnaye. Ho! Ho! She-Buffalo! Ho! Kinsella—

All. Long live Shabnaye! Long live Shabnaye! Shabnaye!

Crotty. We come, Shabnaye, commissioned by the town

    To give to you true and eternal thanks.

    We give you houses, horses, money, lands.

    The White Man's heart is ever with Shabnaye.

Shabnaye. I thank you and I always fight for White man.

    Enter Teresa, Stanislaus, Constantia and Irene.

    Shabnaye! we come to tender you our thanks.

    You have saved us, our pupils, and our friends.

    Whilst life remains, we shan't forget Shabnaye.

    And thanks She-Buffalo.

Shabnaye.   I fight for Black Gown.

Crotty. Here, Sister, are the four whom you have missed.

Teresa. A Colonel, Ellie Laura, looks for you—

    I think it is for you.

Ellie Laura.   I cannot speak,

    So sad am I.

Teresa.   A father seeks a child.

Crotty. What says he?

Teresa.   Ellie Laura is her name.

Ellie Laura. Where does he hail from?

Theresa.   Hails from Avondhu.

Ellie Lauri. Did he have other children?

Teresa.   Yes. Two sons.

Ellie Laura. Where are these children?

Teresa.   Dead.

Ellie Laura.   Where is his wife ?

Teresa. His wife is buried close by Avondhu.

Ellie Laura. Good God ! what is his height, his form, his
    size,

    His age, complexion, color, features—

Crotty.   Stop.

    To-day we come to thank the brave Shabnaye ;

    Sing for the chief, if such be thy desire.

    That colonel in Columbia's name will come

    To thank the great, the good, the brave Shabnaye !

Song.

Ellie Laura. Oh ! had I but the one that I see ;

    Oh ! how quickly my sorrows would flee,

    And how blithe and how happy I'd be,

    And I would fain rejoice !

    Oh ! had I but the joy that I know ;

    Oh ! how sweetly my song would then flow,

    And still younger and younger I'd grow,

    Till I knew father's voice !

Enters the Colonel.

Colonel. Shabnaye ! big chief, protector of the whites,

    I come to express the gratitude of all.

    Hear ! The Great Father speaks from Washington.

    Here are his thanks, his presents to Shabnaye.

Shabnaye takes the presents.

    Shabnaye has never yet the whites betrayed—

    Shabnaye was never yet of foes afraid—

Shabnaye his rank and name will ne'er degrade—
Shabnaye will be Shabnaye, though presents fade!
Ellie Laura is led by the hand and presented to her father by
Sister Teresa. Colonel! thy long lost daughter, thy loved
   child,
I here present to thee. Thanks to Shabnaye—
Or rather thanks to God, who, through Shabnaye,
Hath saved the Whites, and after many years
Of sundered feelings, deep sighs, and saddened hearts,
Restores unto the father from the wild
His Ellie Laura, long lost orphan child,
Pure, spotless, loving, lovely, undefiled.

EPILOGUE.

Some love to roam in lands of peace—
In lands of glory and of lore ;
Some praise the hills and isles of Greece
That look magnificent and hoar.
Enriched with legendary store,
Rome rises grandly o'er the rest,
Since her proud Egale fluttered o'er
Orient, Afric, and the West,
Fierce, fiery, matchless, and supreme confessed.

Still lives America with spells,
And envies not these ancient lands :
In her God's architecture dwells,
Nor mars the mimicry of hands—
There is a spell where mountain stands
Joined with the dark and deep ravine,
Or where the prairie plain expands,
Sad, solemn, sombre, and serene,
Enriched with streams, and garmented with green.

Proud land ! I love thy storms and flood—
Hark ! where thy mighty mountains rise,

Magic in might and multitude ;
Or where thine azure ample skies
Throw their bright canopies
High o'er thy vasty realms all gay.
Elate we see with gladdened eyes
Rude nations from these lands decay,
Though theirs was once Shabnaye—the brave Shab-
    naye!

Enlightened hearers, here we pause,
Rest, spirit of the brave Shabnaye!
Ellie—sweet Ellie Laura's cause,
Still westward moves, as moves the day,
And sounds, where sounded songs of brave Shabnaye.

www.ingramcontent.com/pod-product-compliance
Lightning Source LLC
Chambersburg PA
CBHW022206020726
47496CB00008B/2902